Pedro's Pals

Written by:

Carol McGinnis Yeje

Photography by:

Lisa Duke Boling

Pedro's Pals

ISBN: 978-1-304-50128-8

Published by:

Carol McGinnis Yeje

P. O. Box 175

Roswell, GA 30077

yeje@yahoo.com

Contents:

[Narrator: PEDRO]

Introduction:

As life happens--regardless of the challenges--God's Creations hold 'hope' and 'healing' if we just focus on their amazing beauty.

Lisa took these beautiful pictures when developing a walking routine after a major surgery.

Our connection to each other is strong...through family, friends, and Faith--AND, as Lisa shares, our connection to 'Creation' is strong...through presence and pictures.

Enjoy God's Gift to us--embrace

**'Peace', 'Hope', and 'Healing' through 'pictures'!**

Chapter 1:

Meet My Pals

My name is Pedro.

I live on a farm in Georgia.

I want you to meet my Farm Pals.

This is 'Halo'...one of the beautiful white horses on our farm.

Cash is one of our senior horses.
He watches over all my pals.

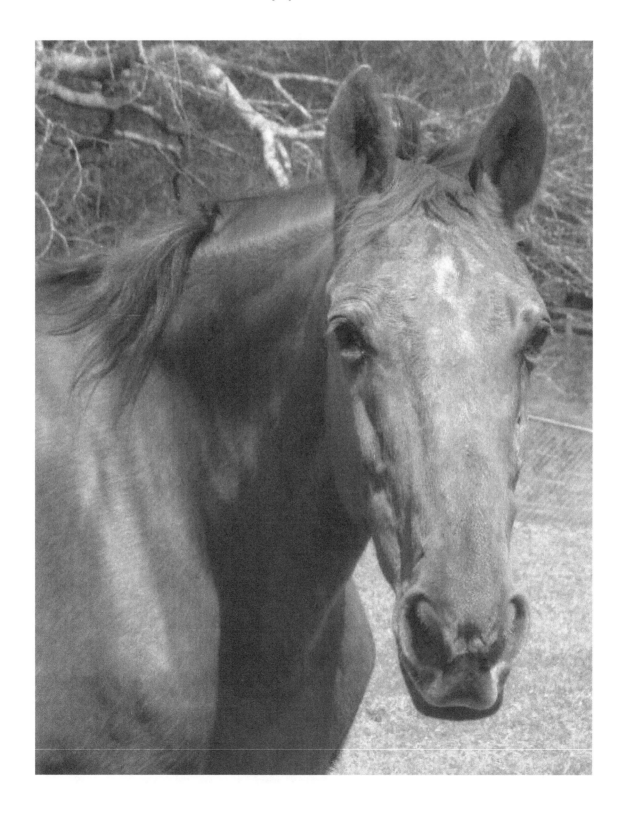

I love to just lay around and watch all the animals.

We also have a mule on the farm.

His name is Festus. He is everybody's buddy.

They are all my buddies, too...I love to hang out with The Beige Buckskin.

He is the best 'grass-patch-finder'.

Yum!

Wow! What a strong body Big Red has. And, so Tall!

Don't know why I have to be short?!

Little Paco, is waiting for his buddies. He's my cousin.

He loves to hide and surprise them!

The two 'paints' [what I call the two-colored horses] are watching Big Red.

They are both so beautiful and strong, too!

Festus looks at him, too.

Look at Majestic...

...and Patches up close.

We've got another 'paint' on the farm, but she's a cow.

I love taking my time...chewing the grass...and talking with all my pals.

Friends are so important to me.

Friends help you enjoy your day.

What are they looking at?

Oh, I see...we have some more young ladies who just arrived.

They always stay together. They are the best of friends.

Festus heads out to the pasture to tell everyone that the young ladies have arrived.

Looks like no one is going to stop eating. Paco, Halo, and The General, are glad to have new arrivals.

No response necessary to Festus.

Big Red asked The General what he thinks of more mouths eating their grass?

Romeo said not to worry. "The young cows eat more hay than grass."

"AND...they are fun to watch..."

"Look...."

Yep. They love that hay.

"Well, they do love grass, too," Paco said.

"See!"

The Beige Buckskin and I are not worried.

Our owners will make sure there is enough for us and all our pals.

Chapter 2:

Pals Watch Out

For Each Other

What is Halo watching?

Cash sees something, too.

Oh, I see what it is...

...it is that big rabbit that visits us sometimes.

Majestic and Festus saw it, too.

Just about that time, Halo comes galloping over the hill...shouting...

'SNAKE! SNAKE!'

"Stay away, Goldie!" Halo shouted.

"Thanks, Halo!" Goldie shouted back.

"Oh, look...there it is!" the horses shouted, together.

"WHERE?" one of the cows shouted.

"I see it...in the tall grass!" The General pointed out.

Most of the animals spotted the snake and stayed away until it wiggled off toward a pond.

Festus shouted back to Halo... "It is gone to the pond. Thanks for the warning!"

"You are welcome!" Halo shouted back. "We all have got to watch out for any danger to any of us."

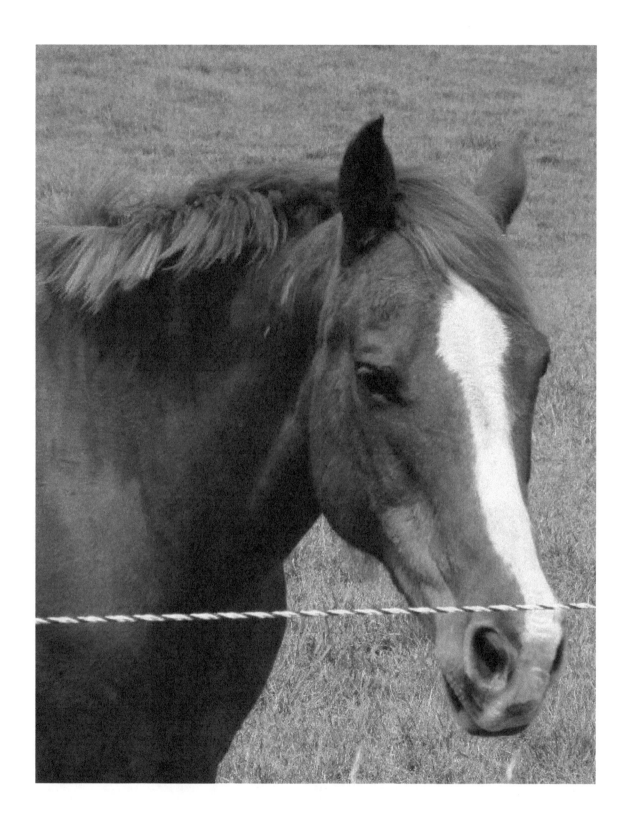

Big Red asked the new young ladies if they saw the little fox that has been roaming around the pasture.

"We have not," they said.

"I saw it," said Betsy.

"I have been looking at this beautiful flower," one of the calves said. "I did not see a fox."

"Oh...there it is...walking away from us," the calf continued.

"Wow! He's a cute little fella'. I see him, now!"

"Do you know of any other critters we should watch out for, Big Red?

AND, are they friendly critters?"

"Well, yes...have you seen the groundhogs?
Look...there's one!"

"There's another one that hides," Big Red replied.

"Look! There one is!" Big Red said.

"That's the bashful one."

The calves said, "We see him!

"Yeah...that's Murray and Henry," I said. "There's another one named Henrietta. I think she's Henry's sister."

Little Paco is focusing on eating.

He doesn't want to talk anymore.

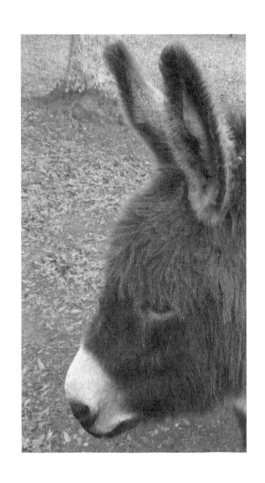

Chapter 3:

Murray, Henry, and Henrietta

"I think I see one of those groundhogs," a calf shouted.

"Watch out for their 'holes'," an older, wise calf said.

All my pals know to watch out for the holes....

"Yeah...and we know to watch out for their feet!"
Murray said.

Paco said, "I didn't know to watch out for your ground-houses... sorry!"

"I'm dodging feet all the time," said Henry.

"Henry is always watching out for feet, for me,"
Henrietta said.

"Yeah," Murray said, as he munched a fig cake.
"Feet can be a problem!"

"Where's my cake?" Henry asked.

"I saw one. Get out and look," said Murray.

"OK...I'll look," Herman replied.

"Got it...thanks!" Henry said.

"Now let's get back to 'feet'," Murray shouted.

Murray finished his fig cake and came out to talk to the pals again--"Could you all be more careful... please!"

"It would help us if everyone would just be more careful where they run," Murray continued.

"We will," said Patches and Majestic.

"OK...me, too," said Big Red.

Festus nodded that he would too.

"We will all watch out more," one of the cows said.

"We don't run much, but we'll look down more."

"You are all wonderful! Thanks for caring!" Murray
said.

Henry said, "Yeah, thanks to all the pals!"

"We really are 'Blessed' to have such caring friends," Murray said.

"Yeah. Now if they could just bring us fig cakes, like our friend Lisa, does," Henry sighed.

Chapter 4:

Parade of 'The Masks'

Sometimes in the spring and early summer, our owners put on our masks to protect us from active insects around our eyes.

Even Majestic gets one.

Cash is used to wearing a mask.

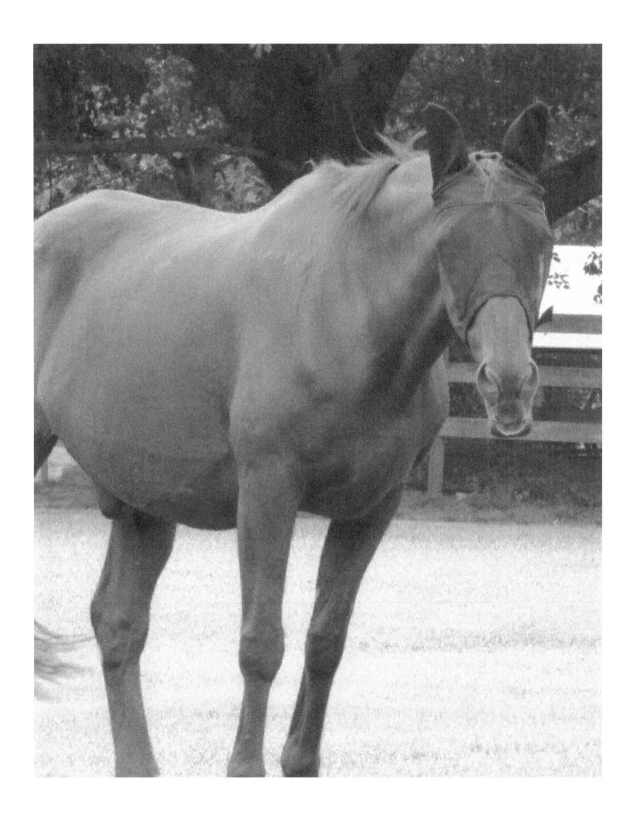

Big Red's tail is too short to reach his face to 'shoo' flies away. He's more comfortable in his mask.

Most of the horses have short tails. They get really tired of having to twist to reach their face with their tail.

Goldie prances around like the mask is a new hat or something.

I guess it feels good not to have the insects continually biting at her face.

Deuce loves the mask, too.

Even The Beige Buckskin wears a mask.

The white horses get white masks.

It's a fashion statement!

I guess the owners ran out of white masks when it was Rosie's turn.

She doesn't seem to mind.

Sometimes Cash wears a blanket.

Some wear a blanket and a mask.

Paco gets a mouth-mask.

I do too. Guess we eat too much?

It's a happy day when the masks are removed.

Goldie celebrates by rolling in the grass!

George saw Goldie…

George shouts, "That looks like fun!"

So, George rolled, too!

Chapter 5:

Birds, Bunnies, and Beauty

We love to watch the geese.

They eat bugs on the ground while walking to the water.

One of our favorite ways to spend the day is to watch the geese and ducks swimming in the lake.

We especially love to watch the babies.

The parents watch out for any danger to their baby.

But, sometimes the 'little one' just slips away from them.

See...there he goes...

"You better come back, little fella'," I shouted.

He turned and started swimming back.

I'm happy he didn't go too far. I saw that little fox in the pasture.

He looks tired and hungry!

There's a buzzard that lands on a pole and checks for food.

Festus chases him away all the time, if he tries to land in the pasture.

"Thanks, Pedro," the parents shouted back to me.
"And, thank Festus for us, too!"

"You are welcome," I shouted. "We love watching your babies!"

There are the duck babies...

They love swimming with mama.

Oh, no...looks like one got left. That little one is calling, "Mama!"

There are 'tuxedo' ducks, I call them.

White ducks...

And some 'different' ducks...

The 'Mallard' Ducks are beautiful.

"We love watching the bunnies, too," said Clorox.

We have several bunnies that visit the farm.

The little bunnies are so cute!

Mr. Turtle is steady, not fast. The bunny loves to watch him.

"Yeah. And we love the beautiful flowers," said Festus.

"My favorites are the ones that the butterflies love," Festus continued.

Everyone likes the pink ones.

And, the purple ones!

The calves voted. They said the yellow and orange flowers are their favorites.

And, of course, we see little squirrels all the time.

The squirrels are always busy, gathering food to save in their nests for the winter.

Squirrels are watching for any animal that may want to take their food...like, maybe, Mr. Turtle.

The Beige Buckskin and his friend, Star, said, "We do love watching those little critters!"

We have lots to enjoy every day!

Chapter 6:

We Have The Cows

We have lots and lots of cows.

They have a shelter.

They love to just relax.

And, listen to the stories of the older cows.

Most of the cows are brown. Here's one with a white streak.

Here's our only 'Paint' cow.

"Yeah. Those are our favorites," said Romeo and Patches.

Wonder why? [ha...ha...]

Guess which cows are Paco's favorites?

You guessed it!

He likes the little ones!

"I have a lot in common with the cows," said Romeo.

"I like to lay around in the grass!"

"Me, too," said The Beige Buckskin.

One of the young calves shouted, "All of us Cows like all of you, too!"

"Yeah...we like all the horses, and Festus...," said the striped cow.

"But...we do have our favorites!"

"Yeah...we love the donkeys!", said the ginger-colored cow.

"Pedro is amazing...and a great teacher. Paco is a fast learner."

"That's right!", shouted the young calves. "Pedro taught him to protect us from the coyotes.

They are both our heroes!"

"Our pleasure, ladies," we shouted back to the cows.

"We protect all the pals! We are small, but we're fast and tough!"

I am very proud of Paco.

Chapter 7:

A Farewell Review

Well, I guess we all have to say good-bye. Come and see us sometime when you visit Georgia.

Little Paco is trying to hide.

He hates to see you go.

"Hope to see you again," said Halo, as he heads over the hill.

Pale Rider says, "Thanks for wanting to learn about us!"

The Beige Buckskin is nodding his farewell.

"Don't forget us," said Majestic.

"We will miss you," said Patches.

Festus says, "Take a walk...enjoy all of God's Creation...until we meet again."

"Yeah. And watch where you step," said Murray.

"And carry some fig-cakes with you to share."

The young calves just can't talk right now.

Miss Betsy says,

"Take care of yourself and your pets!"

While we head to the barn...

Think of us and how we depend on all of you!

We'll all be...

watching...

... for you!

All of my pals...

And, of course, Little Paco!

Oh, wait! I just realized….

We don't have to say goodbye …

Just 'see you later'!

You can visit us anytime!

Just open the book!!!

Pedro's Pals

God Bless!

The...End

Acknowledgements
&
Thanks

...to owners of the animals, featured in this book:

Dr. Edward Holton--
    his sons Matt & James
    at All Animals Vet Hospital;

Carolyn Davis;
Patricia Irwin;
Alex Williams;
Janet Duffy; and

Erin Akers &
    Four Winds Equestrian Center

Lisa [Duke] Boling

Lisa is a native of Roswell, Ga. She has one son, Wade, and a 'furry' son, 'Rambo Duke'. Lisa currently resides in Dawsonville, Ga., next door to the beautiful animals she photographed for this book.

Lisa enjoys walking, photography, music, and walking some more. She loves ALL critters!!

Lisa's message to you:

"Life is quite a journey...may you always choose the roads that lead to the Best Scenery..."